Grace the Cove Dragon

by Maddy Mara

Scholastic Inc.

Copyright © 2023 by Maddy Mara
Illustrations by Barbara Szepesi Szucs, copyright © 2023 by Scholastic Inc.

This book is a work of fiction. Names, characters, places, and incidents are either the product of the author's imagination or are used fictitiously, and any resemblance to actual persons, living or dead, business establishments, events, or locales is entirely coincidental.

ISBN 978-1-338-87548-5

10 9 8 7 6 5 4 3 2   23 24 25 26 27

Printed in the U.S.A. 40

First printing 2023

Book design by Cassy Price

1

Grace had been at sleepaway camp for only a few days, but she already loved it. For two whole weeks she would get to do her favorite thing in the world: swim! At this special camp, kids could have coaching sessions in their favorite water sport. Some kids were learning to water ski; others were doing diving, surfing, or wakeboarding. Grace was training in the pool. She was already one of the fastest swimmers on her team. After camp, she'd be unbeatable!

Grace was sharing a cabin with an awesome surfer named Zoe and a champion diver named Sofia. The three girls had very different skills. Their personalities were different, too. But they had one thing in common: They all loved being in the water.

After training ended each day, everyone had free time. Some kids went for hikes in the forest or read in their cabins. But Grace, Zoe, and Sofia always joined the group headed to the small cove near camp.

"You've been in the water all morning," teased

Emily, their counselor, as the girls spread out their towels on the golden sand. "Isn't that enough for one day?"

"No!" Grace, Zoe, and Sofia cried at the same time.

"Who wouldn't want to be here?" Grace gazed around the beautiful cove. The sun hung low in the sky and a soft golden light danced across the water. All around the bay, palm trees swayed in the gentle breeze. Small children ran in wild circles around their parents, and a group of teenagers played ball by the shore. A salty sea smell wafted through the air.

Emily laughed. "I can't argue with that. Okay, you three know the rules. Make sure you stay within sight of the lifeguards, and don't swim past that red buoy."

"Who's coming in?" Grace asked her new friends.

"I might lie here for a few minutes," Zoe said, stretching out on her towel.

"I'll just check out the pier first," Sofia said. "I want to see if the water is deep enough for me to dive off."

"Okay! I'll see you out there," Grace said, standing up.

Swimming in a pool was great. But there was something about swimming in the sea that Grace couldn't resist. She just had to go in! It was like being under a magic spell.

Grace ran across the sand and splashed into the sparkling water. Small waves broke against her legs as she waded out. Even though she had been practicing all morning, Grace still felt excited to swim. The red buoy floated up and down on the gentle waves. Emily had told them not to swim past it. She didn't say not to swim *to* it, though!

Grace turned back to shore. Emily waved and Grace waved back. Then she plunged into the water and began to swim.

Swimming in the sea was way more challenging than swimming in a calm pool. But Grace loved it. Sometimes she swam over the top of a newly forming wave. Other times, when the wave was about to break, she ducked underneath.

Before long, Grace was in a rhythm. Her arms curved through the shimmering water. Her head turned for air. *One, two, three, breathe.*

As she swam, Grace sang to herself. But soon she realized it wasn't just her own singing that she could hear.

Magic Forest, Magic Forest, come explore...

Grace stopped swimming. Treading water, she looked all around. Who was singing about a magic forest out here in the water? Had Zoe or Sofia swum out to join her?

But no one was nearby. How odd! *I must have imagined it*, Grace decided.

The red buoy was just up ahead now, bobbing cheerfully on the waves. A strange feeling bobbed inside Grace, too. *Something magical is about to happen.*

Once again, Grace heard the strange song.

Magic Forest, Magic Forest, come explore.

She was certain she hadn't imagined the music this time. But where was it coming from? The buoy? It seemed unlikely, but she was almost there. She would check if there was a speaker on it somewhere.

Still treading water, Grace looked back at the shore. She waved to Emily again to let her know she was doing fine. Then Grace swam the last few strokes to the red buoy. Her heart beat fast as a new line of the song swirled around her.

Magic Forest, Magic Forest, hear my roar!

What did that mean? Grace had no idea. Grace's fingers made contact with the smooth plastic of the buoy. She swam in place for a moment, waiting. But for what, she wasn't sure. Grace counted to five. Nothing happened. She counted to ten.

Still nothing.

Grace burst out laughing. For a moment there she'd really thought that something magical was about to happen!

I'll swim back to shore and see if Zoe and Sofia are ready to join me, she decided.

Pressing against the buoy, she flipped backward, diving under the water. Bubbles whirled around her, tickling her skin. Grace closed her eyes, twirling as she glided through the frothy seawater.

Was it her imagination, or did the water feel different now? Warmer and somehow softer. When Grace surfaced for air, her eyes widened in surprise. It wasn't just the water that had changed. Everything had!

2

Grace looked back at the shore. A moment ago, the cove had been full of people, swimming and playing. Now there was no one here at all! Even stranger, the parking lot had disappeared. In its place grew a huge forest. Tall trees reached toward the sky, their leaves rustling. The sounds of twittering birds filled the air.

"Where am I?" Grace wondered out loud.

Her voice sounded strange. Louder and more powerful somehow.

A tiny fish popped its head out of the water. It had a purple tail, a pink face, and an orange body and fins.

"Wow," Grace breathed. "You're the prettiest fish I have ever seen!"

The fish wiggled its fins in a pleased kind of way. And then it spoke. "Thank you. And you're the nicest Sea Dragon I've ever met."

Grace laughed with delight. The fish could talk! But it was clearly a little confused. "I'm no Sea Dragon," she explained. "I'm just an ordinary girl. Tell me, little fish—where am I? Everything looks different."

"You're in the Magic Forest," the fish said, flapping its fins and sending shimmering water everywhere. "In the Magic Cove at the edge of the forest, to be precise. My name is FinFin. I am here to help you. Also, you're definitely a Sea Dragon. Just take a look at yourself if you don't believe me!"

Grace looked down and gasped. She was still in the water, but even so, she could see her body was completely different! She was covered with gleaming aqua scales, for one thing. And her legs had disappeared! Instead, she had an elegant fish tail. It swished back and forth, keeping her afloat. Then she caught sight of her face, reflected in the water's surface. Tall ears twitched on the top of her head. She also had horns, shining like mother-of-pearl!

"Can this be real?" Grace asked herself. It all felt like a dream.

"Try roaring, if you still don't believe it," FinFin suggested.

Grace was about to explain that she didn't know how to roar when a funny burbling grew in her chest. She opened her mouth and a huge roar burst from her. It was so loud that a flock of birds in the forest rose into the air like a colorful cloud, twittering in fright.

"Did I do that?" Grace gasped.

"You certainly did," FinFin said, clapping her fins together, even though they made no sound. "And that was nothing! When Sea Dragons roar underwater, it can be heard hundreds of miles away. But there's no time to try that now.

We need to get to the glade. The Tree Queen is waiting for you."

"The Tree Queen?" Grace repeated. This was getting stranger by the minute. "Who's that?"

"The ruler of the Magic Forest, of course!" explained FinFin. "She is the one who called you and the other Sea Dragons to help. There is a big problem with the Magic Cove."

Grace looked around. The sea was beautiful. Here and there rocks jutted out, glowing in the warm sunshine. Graceful palm trees lined the shore. The cove seemed perfect to her.

"What sort of problem?" she asked.

FinFin did a flip, sending sparkling droplets flying. "All I know is that it's something to do with the Fire Queen. She hates water! We must be careful on our way to the glade. The Fire Queen's helpers are the Fire Sparks. They are bad news, believe me."

Grace nodded. Just because she couldn't see a problem didn't mean there wasn't one. "How do we get to this glade?"

"We fly, of course!" FinFin said.

The little fish leapt up out of the water, flapping her fins furiously. Grace expected her to fall back down into the sea. But she didn't. Instead, FinFin began swishing back and forth, flicking her bright tail. She was swimming but in midair!

"Come on," FinFin urged. "We must get going."

"Sorry, but I can't fly!" Grace explained. "Maybe I could swim there?"

FinFin did another twirl. "Of course you can fly. What do you think those wings on your back are for?"

Grace looked over her shoulder. Sure enough, she had two magnificent wings. She felt her heart begin to beat in double time.

Was it really possible that she could fly?

She stretched out her wings and tried flapping them. The water frothed with bubbles.

"That's it!" said FinFin excitedly. "Keep trying!"

Once again, Grace flapped her wings. And this time she rose above the surface of the water! A moment later, however, she crashed back down into the sea. "Are you sure I can't just swim there?" She groaned when she resurfaced.

"Give it another try," FinFin said. "It's harder when your wings are wet. You'll get it next time, I just know."

FinFin was right. This time, when Grace

began to flap, she soared into the air—and stayed there!

"Follow me," FinFin called.

With a flick of her purple tail, the tiny fish flew away, her fins a fluttering blur.

Grace followed. At first, her flying was a bit wobbly. There were a few moments when she flew so low to the water that her mermaid-like tail skimmed the surface. But gradually she got better and stronger. Before long, she was flying up high above the cove.

FinFin and Grace flew across the water toward the tall trees beyond. They had entered the Magic Forest! The air swirled with the rich scent of tropical flowers and fruits. There was another scent, too.

That's the smell of pure magic, Grace decided. It was a smell she could get used to!

FinFin flew lower, darting through the trees. Her purple tail swished from side to side. Grace followed as closely as she could. But it was more difficult flying through a thick forest than over the sparkling sea. She really hoped she didn't get tangled up in a low-hanging branch.

As the forest grew denser and darker, Grace saw pinpoints of light out of the corner of her eye. She felt like she was being watched. Were they fireflies? Then she remembered FinFin had said something about Fire Sparks. Maybe that's what these things were!

Grace was about to ask FinFin when they burst through the dense thicket and came into a clearing. In the clearing was a strange, shimmering light. It looked like some sort of magical force field, swirling with colors. Through the shimmering air, Grace could just make out a garden inside it.

FinFin did a happy little twirl. "We're at the glade!"

Grace reached a paw through the shimmering air. It tingled as it passed through. The air on the other side of the force field was warm.

Grace's eyes widened in delight. She looked at FinFin. "Are you coming with me?"

"No," replied the little fish. "But don't worry, you're about to meet the other Sea Dragons. And we'll see each other again soon."

"Promise?" Grace asked. FinFin already felt like a friend.

"Promise!" FinFin replied.

With a flick of her purple tail, the little fish disappeared through the trees.

"Okay then, here I go," Grace muttered to herself.

She took a deep breath and pushed through the force field. On the other side was a beautiful garden. Grace saw flowers everywhere she looked. Their bright colors lit up the glade and their sweet scent filled the air. Exotic butterflies flitted from blossom to blossom. A jewel-like pond glimmered nearby.

In the center of the glade grew a magnificent tree covered with deep green leaves and ripe-looking fruit. Grace felt calm just looking at the tree. There was something about the strong branches that made her feel safe.

"Isn't this the most amazing place ever?" said a voice.

For the first time, Grace noticed that she wasn't alone in the glade. Two other Sea Dragons hovered nearby! One was the color of coral and the other was a beautiful golden sandy color, flecked with pale blue.

There was something oddly familiar about the dragons. It suddenly clicked. "Zoe? Sofia?" Grace cried.

"Yes! It's me, Zoe!" the sandy-colored dragon said. "Sofia and I just got here as well. We've been practicing our flying and roaring."

The two dragons flew closer and gave Grace a midair wing-hug.

It was unbelievable! Grace's friends from summer camp were also Sea Dragons!

"I always knew camp would be an adventure." Sofia laughed. "But I didn't realize it would be THIS adventurous!"

Grace looked around the glade. "Have you met the Tree Queen yet?" she asked. She had the feeling that they had some kind of mission ahead of them. She was eager to find out what it was.

"No, but I think we're about to," Zoe said. "Look!" She pointed a talon at the tree in the center of the glade.

The tree swayed gently back and forth. Then, as the three Sea Dragons watched in awe, the trunk changed into an elegant woman, dressed in a flowing moss-green gown. The leaves became long hair framing a wise and beautiful face.

Smiling, the figure stretched out her branches to greet them. "Welcome to the Magic Forest, Sea Dragons!" she said in a warm, rich voice. "I am so glad you made it here. We are in need of your help."

Grace flew closer to the great tree. "What is the problem, exactly? I heard it's something to do with a Fire Queen?"

The Tree Queen nodded, her face serious. "I fear so. The Fire Queen is not fond of water, as you can probably imagine. The three Sea Keepers have gone missing. We suspect she is behind their disappearance."

"What are Sea Keepers?" Zoe asked.

"They are the ocean creatures who help keep the seas in balance," the Tree Queen explained. "The three Sea Keepers enter the Undersea Garden every full moon. Together, they must check the Water Watch. This watch is very important and very powerful. It controls the tides and ensures the balance of the water realms. Once a year, on the full moon, they must wind the watch. That full moon is fast approaching. If the Sea Keepers are not there, the Water Watch will not be wound up."

Sofia looked worried. "And what will happen then?"

The Tree Queen sighed and swayed her branches. "I am not sure. It has never happened before. It's possible the Fire Queen plans to drain the seas entirely."

Grace, Zoe, and Sofia gasped. They shared a deep love of the water. It was what had brought them to camp. The idea of anyone destroying the seas was too terrible to imagine!

"We won't let that happen! And we'll find the missing Sea Keepers," Grace said, turning to her friends. "Right?"

"Right," Zoe and Sofia agreed.

The Tree Queen smiled. "I knew I could rely on you, my brave Sea Dragons."

"But where should we start?" asked Sofia. "The sea is huge!"

"It certainly is vast," the Tree Queen agreed. "And you will only be able to rescue one Sea Keeper at a time. You should start by visiting the Diamond Dolphins. One of the missing Sea Keepers is their leader. They might have some clues to help in your search."

Diamond Dolphins! Grace had always wanted to swim with dolphins. And Diamond Dolphins sounded very special indeed.

"But you three will need to be very careful,"

warned the Tree Queen as her leaves rustled. "Do not assume you are safe in the water. The Fire Queen is very clever. We even think that she has found a way to make her helpers, the Fire Sparks, waterproof!"

Grace looked at her new friends. She was glad that she did not have to battle this Fire Queen and her Fire Sparks on her own. She could tell from their expressions that they felt the same.

"I cannot come with you, of course." The Tree Queen waved a branch in the direction of her impressive roots. "But in a certain way, I will be with you. Take one of these each."

The queen stretched out a branch. Three delicate silver chains dangled from it. On each chain hung a white shell, shaped like a fan. "These shells have special powers," the queen explained. "They will help you in your quest. Wear them, and keep them safe."

Grace took a chain and slipped it around her paw. It was very pretty. Wearing it made her feel calm and somehow even more powerful. She wasn't sure what the shell actually did, but she could sense its magic.

Grace turned to the Tree Queen, about to thank her. But the queen had begun transforming back into a tree. Her hair re-formed into leaves. Her beautiful gown was once again a mossy tree trunk.

"Please, how will we find the dolphins?" Sofia asked quickly.

"Head for Dolphin Cove," the Tree Queen said, her voice so soft it was difficult to hear. "And don't worry, the dolphins will find you. Remember, my Sea Dragons—work together and trust your instincts!"

With that, the Tree Queen's friendly face disappeared.

4

"Dolphin Cove," Zoe repeated. "Either of you know where that might be? I arrived in the Magic Forest at a surf beach. I don't think that's where we're meant to go."

"I arrived here in a lagoon," Sofia said. "It was so beautiful! But it wasn't a cove."

"I arrived at a cove," Grace said.

"That's great!" Zoe said. "Could you find your way back there?"

Grace closed her eyes, trying to remember which way FinFin had led her through the forest. Her mom always said she had a good sense of direction. But there had been so many twists and turns to get to the glade. She wasn't sure if she could find her way back.

Grace felt a tugging at her wrist. Opening her eyes, she saw that the shell on her bracelet had changed. Before, it was plain white. Now it pulsed with an aqua light. And that wasn't all! Grace could hear a voice coming from inside the shell. She held the shell up to her ear.

"I will guide you there, Sea Dragon. Just listen for the ocean," said a voice as gentle as the
waves lapping on the shore.

"My shell is going to show us the way," Grace
said, turning to Zoe and Sofia. "Follow me!"

Together, the three Sea Dragons flew up
and out of the glade and into the vast forest
beyond. Grace held the shell to her ear and the
voice told her when and where to turn. Zoe and
Sofia flew alongside.

"I love surfing in the water," Zoe said, cruis-
ing on a warm gust of wind, "but I have to say,
air surfing is also pretty fun."

"I keep imagining the amazing dives I could

do from way up here!" Sofia laughed, doing a backward somersault.

Grace was enjoying herself as well. Flying felt strangely natural to her. It was sort of like swimming—just with a better view!

"We are almost there," cooed the voice in Grace's shell. Sure enough, Grace could see the tall palm trees and jewel-like cove glittering ahead.

She turned to Sofia and Zoe. "Ready for a swim?"

"You bet!" her friends chorused.

The Sea Dragons flew lower and lower until they were just above the aqua-blue water. Grace and Zoe headed straight for the water, wings tucked in closely by their sides. But Sofia couldn't resist doing a few tumbles and spins as she elegantly dove in after the others.

The warm seawater bubbled all around Grace. She blinked a few times. Usually she needed goggles to open her eyes underwater. But as a Sea Dragon, everything was just as clear down here as it had been in the air. Even better, Grace discovered she could breathe underwater!

She looked around. Beams of sunlight shafted through the bright water, lighting up the underwater world of the cove. Pretty pink, purple, and pale blue seaweed grew like a garden, the delicate tendrils swaying back and forth. Shells of every shape and size decorated the seafloor. Colored fish darted here and there, many of them regarding the three Sea Dragons a little nervously.

"It's so beautiful!" Sofia said with a sigh that sounded like a waterfall.

"Where are these Diamond Dolphins, I wonder?" Zoe mused. "Is your shell telling you anything, Grace?"

"I don't think we're going to need the shell's help." Sofia laughed. "Look!"

A pod of very excited-looking dolphins raced through the sparkling water. Grace loved dolphins and knew a lot about them. But she'd never seen dolphins like these. They looked like they were made from pure silver, etched with delicate swirls. Their fins were as clear as crystal.

"Stay very still," Zoe whispered as the dolphins came closer. "They might be scared of us."

But the dolphins were clearly not afraid! Soon Grace, Zoe, and Sofia were surrounded by chattering silver dolphins. They circled the

Sea Dragons, staring at them curiously.

"Hi! You must be the Diamond Dolphins," Grace said as one dolphin studied her wings in wonder.

"Yes!" replied the nearest dolphin, who had a flower-shaped swirl on her head. "Who are you?"

"We're the Sea Dragons," Grace said. "The Tree Queen sent us. She said that—"

Suddenly the dolphins flapped their tails in alarm.

"Shhhhh!" said the flower-swirl dolphin.

"Don't say anything out here!" cried another. Her dorsal fin flashed red like a warning light. "Follow us to Dolphin City. We can speak in private there."

The pod of Diamond Dolphins flicked their tails and took off.

"Quick! We can't lose sight of them," Grace urged.

Soon she, Zoe, and Sofia were speeding along behind the dolphins. They wove through seaweed gardens, around rocks, and over giant clamshells. Grace had always been fast, but with her new tail, she was faster than ever. She felt like she was flying through the water!

As they passed through a thick patch of sea-weed, Grace kept her eyes fixed on the silver bodies of the dolphins ahead. How far were they going?

A moment later, the Sea Dragons burst out

of the seaweed. Straight ahead was a most remarkable sight. An entire underwater city made from sand! Tall towers rose out of the seabed, dotted with windows, and topped with roofs made from mother-of-pearl. Shell-covered archways joined one tower to the next.

Around every corner and out of every window peeked curious dolphins.

"Wow!" Grace gasped.

"Welcome to Dolphin City," said one of the dolphins, her fin flashing purple with pride. "The finest, happiest city in the cove!" Her face fell. "At least, it was."

"What happened?" Zoe asked, swimming up close.

"You can tell us," said Sofia, coming up on the other side. "We're here to help."

Suddenly, there were dolphins crowding around the Sea Dragons, all speaking in their high voices at the same time.

"Our leader is missing! And he's not just our leader. He's a Sea Keeper."

"He's been kidnapped! Just before the full moon!"

"And we know by who!"

"By the Fire Queen?" Grace asked, thinking back to what the Tree Queen had said.

The Diamond Dolphins began somersaulting in all directions again, their fins changing colors with each turn. It seemed to be what they did when they were upset or excited.

"The Fire Queen? What silly dragons you are! There is no fire in the underwater realm. No, he was kidnapped by the Shiver Sharks!"

5

Grace, Zoe, and Sofia exchanged a look. Shiver Sharks sounded kind of scary. Even the name made Grace ... well ... shiver!

More and more dolphins appeared from the sand-colored buildings of the city. They swam around, their fins changing from blue to purple to neon pink and back again.

"What's going on?" one of the new arrivals asked.

"These courageous Sea Dragons are going to battle the Shiver Sharks!" said the flower-swirl dolphin.

"Ummm, are we?" Sofia whispered, looking at Zoe and Grace. "I don't remember us saying that!"

"You are really brave," said a tiny dolphin, pressing up against Grace's flank. "The Shiver Sharks are sooo big. And they have sooo many teeth! But don't worry. If they eat you, we'll create a dolphin dance in your honor. Or maybe we'll build a sand sculpture for the center of our city."

Grace felt her insides tighten. It took a lot to scare her. But battling huge sharks did not sound easy. Or fun!

"Don't worry about the Shiver Sharks," said a soft voice from nearby. "They are not nearly as scary as dolphins say."

Grace turned to see FinFin. "You're back!" she said.

"Of course," said the little fish. "I will always be here when you need me."

Grace felt her nerves slip away. She turned to the dolphins. "We will not get eaten by Shiver Sharks," she said firmly. "But it sounds like we need to go and talk to them."

The Diamond Dolphins backflipped again

and cheered in their high, squeaky voices.

"We'll take you part of the way," said a few of the bigger dolphins. "Follow us!"

The dolphins led the way through the sandy buildings of their city. As they swam, streams of bubbles trailed alongside their smooth, shining bodies. More dolphins joined the group, swimming out of the doorways and windows of the city.

They were the most amazing creatures Grace had ever encountered!

Gradually, the impressive buildings of Dolphin City thinned out. The farther they swam, the darker and colder the water became. Grace was pleased FinFin was with them.

"Am I imagining it, or are we going deeper?" Sofia asked.

"I thought that, too," Zoe commented, swimming closer. "Hey, something's bugging me. Why would sharks kidnap a dolphin? Doesn't that seem a little weird to you?"

Grace was about to reply when a flash of light streaked past.

"What was that?" She blinked in surprise.

"I don't know," Sofia said, "but here comes another one!"

Another dazzling gleam whooshed by. This time it brushed against Grace's wing. Ouch!

"It's those nasty new fish again!" chattered the dolphins.

"Be careful, they sting! And they make your thoughts all fuzzy."

Grace shook her head. "They're not fish. They have no eyes or tail! And they are hot, like fire."

"Wait," Zoe said, "didn't the Tree Queen say something about waterproof Fire Sparks?"

"You're right!" Grace exclaimed, flapping her

wings. "That's what they are! How do we fight waterproof fire?"

"I don't know," Sofia said grimly. "But we'd better figure it out soon."

A cluster of glowing orbs appeared from the depths of the seabed. More Fire Sparks!

The dolphins swam in panicked circles, squeaking with alarm and trying to beat off the Fire Sparks with their strong silver tails. Their dorsal fins flashed all the colors of the rainbow. The water grew uncomfortably warm as the sparks swam this way and that.

As Fire Sparks surrounded Grace, she felt suddenly confused. What kind of creature had she and her friends become again? And what were they doing here exactly? Her thoughts were all mixed up.

"It's the Fire Sparks," FinFin whispered in her ear. "They make it hard to think straight."

Grace looked over at her friends. Were they feeling muddled like her? Sparks swarmed around Zoe. She let out a frustrated roar, sending a stream of bubbles swirling. The sparks went flying. Some of them went out completely, like spent light bulbs.

"That worked! Let's roar together!" Grace called as another swarm of bright lights darted toward them. "One, two, three!"

The three Sea Dragons roared at the same time. Multicolored bubbles whirled around them, sending Fire Sparks tumbling in all directions.

Right away, Grace's head felt a little clearer. She and her friends were Sea Dragons. And for some reason, they were trying to help the Diamond Dolphins.

"Watch out. They're coming back!" FinFin warned, swishing her tail.

Fire Sparks swam toward them from all directions.

"Okay, Sea Dragons," Grace called to her friends, "time for our biggest roars yet!"

As the Fire Sparks approached, Grace breathed in deeply. She thought about her last swim meet. She had cheered for her teammates in the relay until her voice was hoarse. She tried to summon the same mix of excitement and willpower now. There was no way she and her friends were going to let these sparks beat them!

Once again, on the count of three, Grace roared with all her might. And the louder she roared, the louder Zoe and Sofia roared with her.

Soon the water was so thick with multicolored bubbles she could barely see Zoe and Sofia next to her.

"We did it!" Zoe cried triumphantly. "They're gone. Tail clap, everyone!"

The three friends laughed as they somersaulted and slapped their tails together over their heads.

Grace's mind felt crystal clear. They needed to find the missing Sea Keeper, and they were off to meet—or possibly battle—the Shiver Sharks.

Suddenly, a high-pitched cry went up from the dolphins. They began chattering at the tops of their squeaky voices.

"The Shiver Sharks are coming!"

"Get out of here!"

A moment later, the dolphins had disappeared. Grace's pulse thudded. There, swimming up from the murky depths, was a group of enormous sharks.

6

The sharks silently swam closer. The closer they got, the more Grace wanted to swim off with the dolphins! But she reminded herself that she was a Sea Dragon. Just thinking that made her feel braver. She took a deep breath.

"Stay calm," FinFin reminded her gently.

Grace nodded, but it wasn't easy when there were sharks approaching! She knew nerves were not such a bad thing. She often felt nervous before a swim meet. It helped her think and move fast!

Zoe and Sofia appeared on either side of Grace.

"We've got this," Zoe said steadily. "We're almost as big as those sharks."

"Totally," Sofia agreed. "Plus, we can roar!"

Grace felt a wave of relief. Facing off against a school of Shiver Sharks was the scariest thing she'd ever done. But it was so much better having friends to share in the adventure.

Grace puffed out her chest and spread her wings wide, making herself as big as she could. "Stop right there, Shiver Sharks!" she called. "We need to talk to you."

To her surprise, the sharks stopped instantly. Even more surprising was what happened next. The sharks began to shiver!

"That's weird. Are they cold?" Zoe muttered. "I can hear their teeth chattering."

"I think they might be scared!" Sofia whispered.

Grace stared at the huge creatures. It seemed impossible, but the Shiver Sharks did look like they were trembling with fear.

Grace risked swimming a little bit closer. Instantly, the sharks shrieked and disappeared into the gloomy depths.

"Please don't come any closer!" one of them called in a shaky voice.

"What's wrong?" Grace asked. "You're Shiver Sharks. You're the scariest creatures in the sea!"

One of the sharks, who was speckled with light green dots, came closer. "You have that all wrong. Everyone does. We're not the scariest creatures. We're the most scared ones!"

Grace was so surprised she burst out laughing.

"Don't laugh," said the green-spotted shark. "Everyone we meet says we're terrifying. All the other sea creatures swim off, screaming, when we approach. How do you think that makes us feel? The screaming hurts our ears. And it makes us so jumpy."

"Sorry," Zoe said gently, swimming up beside Grace. "The Diamond Dolphins told us you were scary."

"You shouldn't believe everything you're told," another shark said, sliding up beside the green-spotted one.

"You do look very scary," Sofia added.

"Well, we're not. Shiver Sharks are vegetarians, you know. And we're very shy. We keep trying to invite the dolphins to Shark City for tea and races so they can see that we're not scary. It takes a lot of courage for us to do that. We get so nervous!"

"We hate being rejected," said a sad-looking shark. "Whenever we work up the courage to ask them, they just swim off. It's not very polite!"

"It *is* kind of rude," Sofia agreed. "Poor sharks.

How about we visit your city instead? Would you like that?"

"You mean it?" the spotted shark asked.

A murmur of excitement rippled through the group.

"We've never had visitors before!"

"I would have cleaned up!"

"Will you stay for tea and races?" asked another shark. "We make the best sea tea. And racing is our favorite pastime."

Grace looked over at Sofia. The Shiver Sharks didn't seem very frightening. But did they want to visit a whole city full of them? And did they have time? They had a dolphin leader to rescue.

FinFin murmured in Grace's ear. "It's a good idea. That way you can make sure they don't have the Sea Keeper."

Grace nodded. She did not think the Shiver Sharks had taken the dolphin leader. But FinFin was right. It was a good idea to check.

"This way!" called the sharks excitedly.

They had all stopped shivering. Instead, they swished their tails happily. The three Sea Dragons followed along behind. Grace still felt a little worried. She really hoped this wasn't a trap! But they needed to find the dolphin leader, and visiting Shark City would give them the perfect chance to look.

The sharks led them through the deep water. They swam lower, and the water grew gloomy and dark. Grace noticed something glowing in the distance. It was only faint at first, but the closer they swam, the brighter the glow became. Soon the murky depths of the sea filled with light.

The outlines of buildings began to appear through the water, surrounded by ribbons of bright seaweed.

"It's a city!" Sofia exclaimed.

The buildings themselves were smooth and silvery and radiated a soft twinkle. As the group swam into the city, other Shiver Sharks poked their noses out of windows and around corners. A loud clattering sound rose up.

"It's their teeth!" whispered FinFin.

"Don't be scared, everyone," cried the green-spotted shark as they swam into the center of the city. "We have visitors! They're staying for afternoon tea and races!"

Shyly, the Shiver Sharks began to emerge. "Visitors? No way!" they called to one another excitedly.

"Would you like to try some sea tea? Or perhaps a spicy sharky shake? They have a real bite to them."

"I'll have some sea tea," Grace said politely.

"I'll try a sharky shake," Zoe said.

"Me too." Sofia nodded, although she didn't look at all sure about it.

As the excited sharks swam off to make the drinks, Grace turned to her friends.

"What do you think?" she whispered. "Is it possible that the dolphin leader is here somewhere?"

"I don't think so," Zoe said. "These sharks seem too nice to do something like that."

"Should we look anyway?" Sofia asked.

"Shhh!" warned Grace.

The green-spotted shark was right there, holding a floral teapot in her fins.

"Look for what?" she asked.

"Ummm." Grace was no good at lying. She always thought it was better to tell the truth. "The leader of the Diamond Dolphins is missing. He's a Sea Keeper, too."

"And you think we have taken him?" the shark asked. The teapot quivered in her fins.

"The dolphins told us that it was you," Zoe admitted.

"So that's the real reason you came? I knew it was too good to be true!" The shark started to sob.

Shiver Sharks began appearing from everywhere. They did not look angry. But they did look very upset.

"The dolphins have rejected us again!"

"Worse, the Sea Dragons only visited because they think we're dolphin-nappers!"

"Please don't cry," Grace said. "We love your city! And we don't really think you've taken the Diamond Dolphin leader."

"Of course we haven't taken him." The green-spotted shark sniffled. "Sea Keepers are very important! We'd never do something like that.

We know who did, though. Sharks always know what's going on."

"You do?" Grace asked. "Great! Who took him?"

"We're far too sad to tell you now," said another shark. "You'll have to wait until we're happy again."

"How long will that take?" asked Sofia.

"Forever!" wailed the Shiver Sharks together.

7

Grace, Zoe, and Sofia looked at one another. Who would have thought such big, fierce-looking creatures would be so sensitive?

"What should we do?" Zoe muttered. "We have to cheer them up somehow."

FinFin swished around Grace. "Try distracting them with a game!" she suggested.

Grace smiled. It was a good idea! Games always cheered her up. Turning toward the sharks, she sighed loudly. "I guess you are too sad to have that race."

Instantly, the sharks stopped crying.

"We still want to race!" they called, swishing their tails from side to side.

"Racing is our favorite thing to do!"

"Let's do an obstacle course!"

"Sure," Grace said. "But if we win, do you promise you'll tell us what you know about the missing Sea Keeper?"

"Deal," said the biggest shark. "And if we win, will you come and visit again?"

"Deal!" Grace, Zoe, and Sofia said at once.

"Now, you must choose your fastest swimmer to race against our fastest swimmer."

"Grace, that's you," Sofia said without hesitating.

"Absolutely," Zoe agreed. "I saw you training on the first day of camp. You're the fastest swimmer I've ever seen!"

"Thanks," Grace said. She felt a little quiver of nerves. She knew she was fast—in the human world. But now that she was a Sea Dragon swimming against a Shiver Shark, she had no idea how good she was!

"You can do this." FinFin nudged her gently. "And I'll be with you."

The mood of the Shiver Sharks had

completely changed. None of them looked even slightly sad anymore. They were chatting excitedly, flapping their fins, and swishing their long, smooth bodies.

Then the group parted and a particularly sleek shark moved to the front.

"This is our fastest shark, Smiler," the green-spotted shark said proudly. "He's actually the fastest swimmer in the entire sea. At least, we think he is. No other sea creatures have ever raced against us!"

"He sure looks fast," Grace said. Now she was *really* nervous!

Zoe gave her a quick wing-hug. "You're a Sea Dragon, don't forget. You'll do great."

"We'll be cheering you the whole way," Sofia added, wrapping a wing around the other two.

"Time for the race to begin!" announced the green-spotted shark. "Listen up while I explain the course. First, you must swim through Shark City. Be careful, because if you touch any of the buildings as you pass, you will be disqualified."

Grace gulped. This race was already sounding hard.

"Next is the rock tunnel," the shark continued. "That's where the Snippy Clawed Crabs live. Better speed up through that part. Snippy Clawed Crabs are ... well ... snippy."

"The final stage is the Seaweed Forest.

Watch out for the Stinger Eels. They're hard to spot in all that seaweed. But you sure know if you touch one. They sting!"

"I thought Shiver Sharks were scared of everything," Zoe whispered. "They seem pretty brave to me."

"I know, right?" Sofia said. "Maybe they're only nervous when they're getting to know someone. I'm like that, too."

The spotted shark held up its fins. "Competitors, get ready to race!"

The sleek shark called Smiler swam alongside Grace. Grace felt her stomach flutter. Smiler was so big and powerful! Did she stand any chance of beating him?

To Grace's surprise, Smiler reached out a fin. "I'm so happy that I finally get a chance to race!" he said, showing a broad, toothy smile. "Good luck, and let's have fun!"

Grace took hold of the shark's fin with her paw and gave it a friendly shake. It was clear Smiler got just as excited as Grace did about swimming competitions. It was weird—she had never expected to have something in common with a shark. Then again, Grace had never expected to turn into a Sea Dragon. Life could be very surprising!

"Good luck to you, too!" she said warmly.

"Three, two, one, GO!"

Smiler shot off in a whirl of bubbles. Grace

set off behind him, with FinFin by her side.

"Go, Grace!" yelled Zoe and Sofia.

Swimming through Shark City was tricky. This wasn't just because the streets were narrow and full of sharks. It was also because it was such an interesting place. Everywhere Grace looked, she saw cool buildings, underwater parks, and beautiful sea sculptures. There was even a huge fountain! Pink water flowed from it before merging with the surrounding seawater.

Stay focused, Grace reminded herself, tearing her eyes away from all the sights. She needed to win this race so they could find out about the missing dolphin leader. The Tree Queen was counting on them!

As Grace moved into a wider part of the city, she flapped her wings and glided smoothly ahead. She loved how much extra power her wings gave her. She surged forward, gaining on Smiler. If only she had wings back in the human world!

A large, rocky cliff face loomed ahead. Grace frowned. Was she supposed to swim over that?

Or around it? Then she saw Smiler disappear into a small entrance in the middle of the rock.

"It's the rock tunnel," explained FinFin. "We're going through it!"

It was a narrow squeeze—much too narrow for Grace to use her wings. The tunnel was dark, too, but Grace found that her Sea Dragon eyes could see surprisingly well. Every now and then, a pair of sharp claws reached out and nipped at Grace as she sped by.

"Snippy Clawed Crabs are so annoying," muttered FinFin, swishing her tail away from a claw just in time. But Grace barely noticed their pinches. Her strong scales protected her, for one thing. And for another, her mind was busy thinking about how she could get in front of Smiler.

I can't pass him in the tunnel. I will have to try in the Seaweed Forest.

Up ahead, Grace saw Smiler, his graceful tail gliding through the water.

"He's out of the tunnel!" said FinFin excitedly. "Quick!"

Grace pushed with her mermaid-like tail as hard as she could. A moment later, she burst out of the tunnel and was surrounded by strands of seaweed, gently drifting from side to side. The Seaweed Forest!

Grace stretched out her wings and used them to push forcefully through the water. This was her chance to get ahead! She zoomed into the colorful seaweed. But which way should she go? Even as she thought this, she felt a tug. Looking down, she saw the shell on her bracelet pulsing with aqua light.

As she held it to her ear, the voice said, "Go straight ahead, then to the left."

With another powerful wing flap, Grace shot forward—and zoomed right past Smiler. She was in the lead! Grace neatly dodged an eel hiding among the plants. She felt unstoppable. Dragon power surged through every muscle.

Suddenly there came a loud yell. Grace knew she shouldn't look around. If she wanted to win, she had to focus on the finish line. It wasn't far off! But she couldn't ignore that yell.

Grace risked a look back. Poor Smiler was surrounded by giant eels!

8

Grace stopped. This was the first time she'd been ahead of Smiler. If she kept swimming, she would win. Then they'd find out where the dolphin leader was!

But there was no way Grace was going to leave Smiler to battle the Stinger Eels on his own. She spread her wings and flicked her tail to turn back.

"Come on, FinFin," she called. "We have a friend in need!"

She and FinFin sped back to Smiler, who was shivering badly.

"Y-y-y-you came back to h-h-help?" Smiler gasped, his huge mouth wide with wonder.

"Of course," Grace said. "Stinger Eels look nasty. Much better if we tackle them together."

"Watch out!" FinFin warned.

An eel lashed out at her. Grace just managed to somersault out of the way.

Smiler shivered even more.

"Don't be scared," Grace murmured to the huge shark. "Sure, the eels sting. But we've got each other. And we've got tail power!"

Grace moved her tail in circles, creating a whirlpool effect. As eels approached, the swirling water sucked them in. Soon the eels were spinning around and around!

A huge smile stretched across Smiler's face. A moment later, he, too, was swishing his tail in circles. The whirlpools grew wider and faster. Each time an eel tried to attack, it was caught up in the vortex! It spun around like a sock in a washing machine.

"On the count of three, let's flick them away!" Grace called. "One, two, three—flick!"

Grace and Smiler flicked their powerful tails, sending the eels spinning off into the dark water. They grew smaller and smaller until they vanished completely.

"We did it!" cheered Grace, slapping fins with Smiler. FinFin swam in excited circles around them.

"Are you guys okay?"

The seaweed parted, and there was Sofia, followed by Zoe and some worried-looking sharks. "We heard yelling."

"We're fine, thanks." Grace grinned at Smiler. "We just had to team up against some Stinger Eels. But they were no match for our turbo tails."

"What about the race?" Zoe asked.

"You'll have to start over," said the green-spotted shark.

"There's no need for that." Smiler swam to the front of the group. "This Sea Dragon could have easily beaten me. But instead she chose to help me. She's the winner, as far as I'm concerned."

The sharks formed a huddle, speaking in low, toothy tones. Finally, the green-spotted shark turned and spoke.

"We have voted. We all agree the Sea Dragon won the obstacle course. What's more, you are officially friends of the Shiver Sharks. Now, I'm sorry to tell you this, but if you want to find the dolphin leader, you will have to go some-where very dangerous."

Grace and her friends looked at one another. They'd had just about enough danger for one day!

"Where do we have to go?" Grace asked.

"Up to the surface," said another shark,

dropping his voice. "You must be careful; it's scary up there."

"No, it's not!" Zoe said. "The surface of the water is great. That's where the waves are."

"But it's also where the hot fish are," Smiler muttered.

Some of the sharks begin to shiver.

"The Fire Sparks!" Grace groaned.

"They captured the dolphin leader. We saw them do it with our own eyes!" said the green-spotted shark.

"What happened?" Grace asked.

"We were hiding in the shadows when a pod of dolphins swam past. Suddenly the hot fish appeared. They attacked the dolphins! We were scared, but we swam over to try to help."

"That was very brave," Zoe said kindly.

"Maybe, but the dolphins just panicked when they saw us. Like they always do. There was so much chaos, they didn't even see their leader being taken. But we did!"

Grace nodded grimly. This all made sense.

"Do you want us to take you up there?" asked the green-spotted shark. Grace could feel her nerves. Once again, Grace found it strange to know such powerful creatures could be so fearful!

Grace's shell gave a gentle tug, reminding

her it was there to help. "No need. We can find the way."

The Sea Dragons said goodbye to the Shiver Sharks and thanked them for their help.

"Our pleasure," the sharks called as Grace and her friends swam up and away. "Come back whenever you like."

The higher the Sea Dragons swam, the warmer the water grew. Rays of pink and orange light filtered through.

"The sun is starting to set," Sofia observed, swimming alongside Grace.

Grace nodded. She really hoped they found the dolphin leader before nightfall.

For a moment, Grace felt her nerves return. What lay ahead, waiting above the surface?

"You just made friends with sharks," FinFin reminded them. "Whatever is waiting up there, you three can deal with it."

"Thanks, FinFin," Grace said. The little fish had a way of making her feel better.

Kicking and flapping with all their might, Grace, Zoe, and Sofia burst through the surface and took their first gasps of air in a long time.

Above the water, the cove looked beautiful. Everything was bathed in gentle sunset colors. There was only one thing that wasn't perfect, and it took a moment for Grace to understand what she was seeing. That's because hovering in midair was…a dolphin! *How was the dolphin staying in the air? And didn't the poor thing need water?* Thick clusters of Fire Sparks were looping around and around the dolphin, like buzzing comets orbiting a planet. One thing was for sure: There was strange and powerful magic at play.

9

"The dolphin leader!" Sofia gasped.

"It must be," Grace agreed.

"How is he trapped like that? And how are we going to rescue him?" Zoe wondered aloud.

Grace had been wondering the same thing. She'd never seen so many Fire Sparks in one place!

The dolphin happily waved a fin at Grace and her friends. Strangely, he did not look worried. He just looked a little … puzzled.

"Don't worry!" Grace called above the hum of Fire Sparks. "We're going to rescue you!" To her friends, she muttered, "We just need to figure out how. Any ideas?"

"Maybe we could pull the Fire Sparks away from the dolphin with our sharp claws?" Sofia suggested.

"Or swish them away with our powerful tails?" Zoe added.

These were good ideas. Carefully, Grace reached out a talon. The Fire Sparks buzzed angrily, making the air crackle with heat and magic. Grace felt a sharp pain in her talon as if she'd touched an open flame.

"Ouch!" she cried, nursing her burned paw. "Hmm. I don't think we can touch them."

"Well, we have to do something because they've spotted us!" Zoe cried.

Sure enough, one group of sparks kept

swirling around the trapped dolphin while a second group broke away. It streaked toward the Sea Dragons like a fiery comet.

"Duck!" FinFin cried in alarm.

The three friends tucked in their wings and dove under the water. But the Fire Spark comet followed them under the surface! The water bubbled and roiled. Even worse, Grace felt herself getting dizzy and confused again.

What were they doing again? Grace tried to clear her thoughts. She was not going to let these pesky sparks confuse her!

We're here to rescue the first Sea Keeper, she reminded herself.

Then, before her confusion could return,

Grace flew up to the surface and surged out of the water and high into the air. Zoe and Sofia followed close behind. In the air, Grace's mind felt clearer. For some reason, the sparks didn't muddle her as much out of the water.

But they were still annoying! The horrible things swarmed around Grace's face, stinging her ears and dazzling her eyes. How could she and her friends beat Fire Sparks that even water could not quench?

Grace roared with frustration, and something very surprising happened. Grace could *see* her roar! It shimmered like a fine, misty, aqua cloud. And as the cloud enveloped the Fire Sparks, they fizzed and disappeared!

Excited about her discovery, Grace called out to Zoe and Sofia, who were swatting at sparks with their wings and tails. "I think our roars have special powers! They can smother the Fire Sparks. Try it!"

Grace watched as Zoe roared, sending a glorious purple mist into the air. Soon it was joined by Sofia's misty orange roar. Their roars blanketed the Fire Sparks. With a splutter, the sparks vanished.

Grace took a deep breath and roared again.

But this time, nothing happened. Her roar did not produce a mist, and it had no effect on the sparks.

Grace's mind raced. *We are Sea Dragons.*
Maybe we need to use the seawater! she
thought.

Grace dove back into the water, then turned
and smoothly launched herself up into the air
again. This time when she roared, her Fire
Spark–squishing mist was back!

Zoe and Sofia grinned when they under-
stood what Grace was doing. They, too, dove
into the water and came back up with fully
charged Sea Dragon roars.

"Keep going!" Grace encouraged her friends.
"It's working!"

Frenzied Fire Sparks zigzagged back and

forth, trying to dodge the misty roars. Grace barely noticed. When she was in a race, she always blocked out the sights and sounds around her and stayed focused on her goal. She felt the same way now.

The Sea Dragons dove back into the water

one last time and surged up, roaring louder than ever. Their misty roars filled the air, forming a huge cloud above the Fire Sparks trapping the dolphin. It closed around the remaining sparks, which hissed and fizzed as they were extinguished.

The dolphin, suddenly free, arced through the air. It flipped gracefully and then plunged into the water below.

10

"We did it!" cheered Grace.

Zoe and Sofia whooped with delight, and little FinFin swished her tail joyfully.

The few remaining Fire Sparks whirled off into the air and flew away, humming with fury.

"Yeah, buzz off, you annoying things," Zoe

called after them, laughing. "Hey, is the Sea Keeper okay?"

Even as she spoke, the dolphin poked his nose up above the surface of the water. He gazed around, looking confused. "Where am I? And who are you?"

Before Grace could answer, the water around them began to churn. For a horrible moment, Grace thought the Fire Sparks were back.

But a moment later a silver dolphin snout appeared, etched with swirling designs. Then another snout popped up—and another and another! Suddenly the sea was full of Diamond Dolphins, chattering around their returned leader. They were so excited that their dorsal fins flashed with color.

The Diamond Dolphins circled their leader, squeaking happily. "You are in Dolphin Cove," they reminded him. "The Shiver Sharks kidnapped you. I bet it's because you're a Sea Keeper. But everything is better now that the Sea Dragons rescued you!"

"The Shiver Sharks did NOT kidnap him," Grace called. She had to speak loudly to be heard over the dolphin chattering. "It was the Fire Queen and her Fire Sparks."

"In fact," Zoe chimed in, "the sharks actually helped us. They told us where we'd find your leader!"

"You know, dolphins shouldn't be scared of Shiver Sharks," Sofia added. "They're very friendly."

The Diamond Dolphins looked at one another doubtfully. Clearly, they didn't believe the Sea Dragons.

But then their leader spoke. "It's coming back to me now," he said slowly. "The Sea Dragons are speaking the truth. The Shiver Sharks had nothing to do with my capture." He turned to Grace, Zoe, and Sofia. "And if the sharks helped you find me, then we owe them an apology. Perhaps we should give them a gift. What would they like, do you think?"

Grace smiled. "You know what would make

them really happy? Visit them for afternoon tea and races!"

The dolphin leader's dorsal fin flashed green with pleasure. "Then that is what we'll do. And what about you, Sea Dragons? How can we thank you? Would you like to come for a feast in Dolphin City? We could catch shrimp in your honor. They are delicious eaten raw. And their shells are so very crunchy!"

"That's very kind, but there's no need to thank us. Plus, we have to get home," Grace said hastily. She didn't even like cooked shrimp—she was pretty sure she would not like them raw and with their shells on!

With happy high-pitched goodbyes, the

dolphins leapt into the air and dove back underwater, swimming swiftly away as one big, contented pod.

The Sea Dragons turned to look at one another.

"I wonder *how* we get home," Zoe said, voicing what they were all thinking.

"Maybe we return to the glade?" Sofia suggested.

It was a good idea, but Grace had noticed something. The shells on their bracelets were glowing! Without really thinking, Grace took hers off and cupped it in her paws. Zoe and Sofia did the same. The shell quivered in Grace's paws, and she felt it pulling toward the other two shells like magnets being drawn together.

"They're joining up," Sofia observed.

When the three shells touched, there was a satisfying click and a sudden burst of light. When the light faded, the three shells had formed into one beautiful pearly shell.

"Look!" Zoe pointed. "There's something in it!"

Zoe was right. An image flickered on the shell's smooth surface. A moment later, the glade appeared on the shell.

The Tree Queen's elegant face appeared, smiling broadly. "Thank you, Sea Dragons," she said in her warm, rich voice, "for rescuing the first Sea Keeper. You did very well on this first quest."

"This *first* quest?" Grace leaned forward eagerly. "You mean, we get to come back? There will be more quests?"

"That's right. Sea Dragons, your work here is not yet done," the Tree Queen said, her branches swaying. "What do you say? Will you three return to help rescue the other missing Sea Keepers?"

Grace thought about their adventure. She and her friends had flown high in the sky. They'd swum deep underwater with wild sea creatures. They'd even battled the Fire

Sparks—and won! Best of all, they'd rescued the dolphin leader.

"Grace, you're shivering like a Shiver Shark." Sofia looked worried.

"Are you nervous about something?" Zoe asked kindly.

Grace laughed. "I'm not shivering from nerves. I'm shivering from excitement!" She turned to the Tree Queen. "I'd love to come back again. And I'm pretty sure Zoe and Sofia would, too, right?"

"Definitely!" Zoe and Sofia cried together.

"I am pleased to hear it." The Tree Queen nodded gently. "Now, you each have your own path home. Pull the shells apart, and hold your own to your ear. I will explain to each of you the way ahead. Until next time!"

The image of the Tree Queen and her glade faded, and suddenly the shell looked like an entirely normal shell once more.

Grace wasn't sure how to separate the shells. They had fused into one! But when each Dragon Girl gave their piece a gentle tug, they easily clicked apart.

Grace held hers to her ear. She heard the rhythmic sound of the sea, and then she heard the Tree Queen speaking.

"Dive into the water," the Tree Queen instructed, "and swim away from the setting sun, toward the shore. And remember, keep this shell with you at all times. It will tell you when it's time to return."

"Okay, I will!" Grace promised.

"Goodbye, Grace. You have successfully led the first quest!" The Tree Queen's voice faded away and the sound of the sea returned.

Grace turned to FinFin, the little creature who had been such a help and comfort throughout their adventure. "Thank you a million times over for your help!"

"Goodbye, Sea Dragon," said the brightly colored fish. "It was a pleasure getting to know you." With a flick of her purple tail, FinFin dove into the water.

Grace wrapped Zoe and Sofia in a huge wing-hug. "I'll see you back at camp!" she said. Then, taking a big gulp of air, she dove underwater and began swimming.

The warm salt water streamed past Grace as she swished her tail and used her powerful wings once more to swim as fast as she could. As she headed for the shore, she spotted dolphins and even glimpsed a Shiver Shark hiding behind tendrils of seaweed.

But as she swam, the magical cove gradually faded away. The water became bluer and cooler. Grace burst through the water's surface, breathing in deeply. Dolphin Cove had vanished and she was right next to the red buoy! Even more amazing: It seemed like no time had passed in the normal world.

Grace was back in her human body. She reached a hand into the air and wiggled her fingers. For a moment, Grace felt a pang of sadness. It had been so cool being a Sea Dragon! And it had been amazing to visit the Magic Forest.

Then she saw the shell bracelet on her wrist. *We get to go back!* she reminded herself.

"Grace!"

Zoe and Sofia jumped up and down on the beach, waving. Grace grinned and waved, too. That was the other good thing. She still had camp and her new friends to keep her busy.

"Coming!" she called. Then, turning one last time toward the open sea, she murmured, "See you again soon, Magic Forest!"

Turn the page for a special sneak

peek of Zoe's adventure!

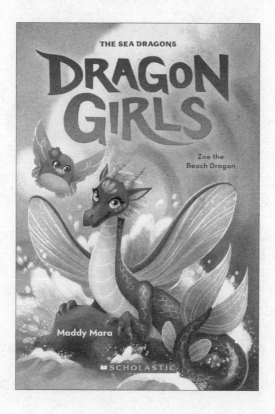

1

Zoe sat on her yellow surfboard, floating on the water. She scanned the horizon. Were there any good waves coming?

Zoe had been going surfing with her dad and big sister ever since she was really small. Riding a surfboard felt almost as natural as walking. She loved being out in the glittering sea, waves breaking around her. It was amazing how all Zoe's worries disappeared when she was on her board. Nothing beat the feeling of riding a wave all the way to shore! Zoe could do it all day.

That's why Zoe's mom had suggested sleep-away aquatics camp this summer. Zoe had jumped at the idea! So far, camp had been as good as she'd hoped. In fact, it had been way better. For one thing, she got to surf every day. For another, there were so many great kids to get to know. Zoe got along with most people. But she had formed a special bond with her cabinmates Grace and Sofia.

All these things combined to make camp fantastic. But there was something else.

Something that made it . . . magical. Zoe, Sofia, and Grace had found out that they were able to travel to another realm. It was called the Magic Forest. When they were there, they became dragons. Not just ordinary dragons, either. Sea Dragons, to be exact!

The three new friends had already had one adventure in the Magic Forest. They had helped the Tree Queen, who was the ruler of the Magic Forest, by rescuing a missing dolphin. Acing the quest had felt incredible, and the Tree Queen told them she would need their help again. Zoe could hardly wait to return. She was glad that she had surfing to keep her mind busy until that happened!

Every day at camp, Zoe went with the other surfing kids to the local surf beach. Their coach, Stef, surfed alongside them, giving them tips to improve their skills. Zoe had already learned so much.

Zoe did not see her new friends during the day, because Grace was a swimmer and Sofia a diver. This meant they each had different activities in other locations. But that was fine. It was fun talking about their days when they caught up every afternoon.

Today, Zoe had already been in the water for an hour. But it felt like only a few minutes.

Up ahead, she spotted a wave beginning to swell. Zoe started to paddle, getting herself into a good position as she waited for the wave to build. When Zoe was surfing, everything else dropped away. She thought about just two things: the board beneath her and the movement of the water around her.

"Get ready, Zoe!" called Stef from nearby. "That wave is going to be huge!"

It was time. Zoe sprang up onto her board. She landed perfectly, crouching low, her left foot forward. She started coasting along the lifting wave. Foamy white droplets splashed down over her as the wave began to curve. Zoe could hear the swell of the ocean all around her, the waves crashing on the shore. But she could hear something else, too.

Magic Forest, Magic Forest, come explore . . .

Excitement bubbled in Zoe—and it wasn't about the perfect wave she was riding. She'd heard that song before. It had been when she traveled to the Magic Forest last time! Was she about to go back? Oh, she hoped so!

The wave Zoe was riding stretched on and on. She felt like she was surfing through a beautiful blue tunnel. Zoe heard the song again. It blended with the sound of the sea itself.

Magic Forest, Magic Forest, come explore.

Zoe stretched out a hand and trailed it along the wave. Her silver bracelet with its fan-shaped shell glinted on her wrist. The Tree Queen had given one each to Zoe, Grace, and Sofia. Usually the shells were white. But right now, Zoe's glowed pale aqua.

Zoe's heart thumped. She was sure of it. She was about to be sent on her second magical quest! She had a feeling that this quest would be even harder than the first. But that probably meant it would be even more exciting. Then she heard the final line in the song.

Magic Forest, Magic Forest, hear my roar!

Zoe grinned. She loved roaring when she was a dragon. It was such a powerful, freeing feeling. She couldn't wait to do it again.

Finally the wave crashed, pulling Zoe off her board. Zoe went with the flow and closed her eyes. She hoped that when she opened them again, she would be in a very different place!

2

Zoe rose to the surface of the water and burst through. Air filled her lungs and the sun warmed her face. She hadn't opened her eyes yet. Had she been transported into the Magic Forest? She hardly dared to look! The water felt softer and warmer. And the waves sounded different somehow. Rather than crashing, they made a magical tinkly sound. It reminded Zoe of wind chimes, blown by a summer breeze.

Zoe opened her eyes. Looking around, she saw she was still at a surf beach. But it was not the same one she'd just left. All the other surfers in her group had disappeared. The people who had been sitting on the beach were gone, too. Before, there had been beach shacks lining the shore. Now the shacks had been replaced with tall trees.

A shiver of excitement passed through Zoe. *The Magic Forest!*

Treading water, Zoe glanced down at herself. She grinned at what she saw. Yes! She was back in her dragon form! Her body was covered with sandy yellow scales, tipped with blue. She had a long, swishy tail that made treading water as easy as breathing. She also had a fabulous pair of wings. Zoe gave them a huge flap and rose smoothly out of the water.

She zoomed up, sending shimmering droplets of water in every direction. Surfing would always be Zoe's first love. But flying was a very, very close second.

"Flying is like surfing in the air, isn't it?" said a friendly little voice.

Zoe looked down. Swimming in the sea below her was the tiniest penguin Zoe had ever seen. It looked up at Zoe with big blue eyes.

"Hello there. Yes, that's exactly what it's like!"

agreed Zoe, swooping around and coming back to hover near the tiny penguin. A thought crossed her mind. "But how do you know that? I know that penguins can surf. But they can't fly, can they?"

Instead of answering, the penguin flapped its stubby little wings furiously. To Zoe's great surprise, the penguin flew up into the air beside her. Even more surprising was how the tiny creature looked. Zoe had never seen a purple-and-white penguin before!

"I'm a pixie penguin," explained the bird. "My name's Splashi."

"Hi, Splashi! I'm Zoe," Zoe said. "I'm a Sea Dragon."

Splashi did a twirl. She had a funny way of flying. Her whole body seemed to waddle. But Zoe was careful not to laugh. She didn't want to hurt the little bird's feelings.

"Oh, I know that!" said Splashi. "I've been waiting for you to arrive. The Tree Queen wants me to bring you to her as quickly as possible. She really needs help from you and your friends."

"Let's go, then!" Zoe said.

Surfing had taught Zoe to act quickly. And she wanted to leap into this adventure as soon as possible.

Together, Splashi and Zoe flew over the sparkling sea toward the huge trees of the Magic Forest. A strong wind blew in from the shore.

It almost felt as if it was trying to stop them from getting to the Magic Forest.

"The wind is part of the Fire Queen's magic," Splashi explained. "She was furious when you and the other Sea Dragons rescued the first Sea Keeper. She is determined to stop you from rescuing the others."

Zoe flapped her wings harder than ever. The Fire Queen could make the strongest winds she wanted. There was no way a bit of hot air was going to stop the Sea Dragons!

ABOUT THE AUTHORS

Maddy Mara is the pen name of Australian creative duo Hilary Rogers and Meredith Badger. Hilary and Meredith have been making children's books together for many years. They love dreaming up new ideas and always have lots of projects bubbling away. When not writing, Hilary can be found cooking weird things or going on long walks, often with Meredith. And Meredith can be found teaching English online all around the world or daydreaming about being able to fly. They both currently live in Melbourne, Australia. Their website is maddymara.com.

DRAGON GAMES

PLAY THE GAME. SAVE THE REALM.

READ ALL OF TEAM DRAGON'S ADVENTURES!

Collect them all!